Sam's Windy Day

Sarah and James decide to fly their kite in the park but things don't go the way they planned . . .

SAM'S WINDY DAY

**Written and drawn
by Rob Lee**

Filmset in Nelson Teaching Alphabet
by kind permission of
Thomas Nelson and Sons Ltd.

Fireman Sam copyright © 1985 Prism Art and Design Ltd.
Fireman Sam is a stop-frame animation series
commissioned by S4C. Produced by Bumper Films.
All rights reserved throughout the world.

© 1986 Prism Art and Design Ltd.
Published in Great Britain by World International Publishing Limited,
An Egmont Company, Egmont House, P.O. Box 111,
Great Ducie Street, Manchester M60 3BL.
Printed in Italy.   SBN 7235 7939 3

One morning Sam was getting ready for work. "I'm a bit early," he said, as he picked up the telephone. "I'll give Sarah and James a call."

But the telephone wasn't working!

"That's odd," said Sam. "It was working yesterday."

"Never mind, I'll have time to pop into Bella's Cafe for my sandwiches," said Sam, as he checked in the mirror that his buttons were shiny and his helmet was at a suitably jaunty angle before leaving. Sam liked to be the smartest fireman in Pontypandy.

However, as soon as Sam stepped out of the house, a gust of wind whipped his helmet off and sent it rolling down the street.

"Great fires of London!" exclaimed Sam. "It's a bit blowy today."

Bella was a jolly Italian lady who owned the cafe in Pontypandy High Street. When Sam arrived he found Bella was having trouble with the telephone, too.

"Now I can't-a-telephone the baker to-a-deliver the bread," said Bella.

"It looks like I'll have to do without my sandwiches," said Sam.

Meanwhile, Sarah and James were heading for the park in Trevor Evans' minibus. James was carrying a brightly-coloured kite.

"It's a lovely windy day for flying a kite," said Sarah.

"Just make sure you keep your feet on the ground!" chuckled Trevor.

Soon they arrived at the park.

"Thanks, Mr Evans," said the children, as they got off the bus.

Trevor leaned out of the window and said, "Perhaps I could get you started. I used to be quite an expert with kites."

Before the children could answer, Trevor had climbed down and unravelled the twine. Then he began running along the street, towing the kite behind him. "How about that then?" said Trevor proudly, in between puffs and pants.

"Be careful, Mr Evans!" called the children.

"Nonsense!" shouted Trevor, looking back at the children as he ran. If Trevor had been looking where he was going, he might have noticed the hole in the road before he fell into it! "OUCH!" cried Trevor as he fell down.

"That's a silly place to put a hole in the road," said Trevor.

"Are you hurt?" asked Sarah.

"I think I've sprained my wrist," replied Trevor. "And it looks like I've lost your kite, too!"

The children helped Trevor out of the hole.

Meanwhile at Pontypandy Fire Station, Station Officer Steele was talking to Sam. "I've had a report of a telegraph pole being blown down in Pandy Lane. We'd better go and see what we can do," said Officer Steele.

"That's why the telephones haven't been working," cried Sam.

Steele and Sam boarded Jupiter, the fire engine, and made for Pandy Lane. Eventually they came across the telegraph pole.

"It's a danger to traffic at the moment," said Steele. "We'd better tow it to the side of the road."

Sam hitched a rope from the engine to the telegraph pole, then climbed aboard the engine and started it up.

"Easy, Sam," called Steele, "left hand down a bit ... right hand ... a bit more, that's it!"

Soon the pole was safely at the side of the road.

"We can leave it to the telephone engineers now," said Steele.

Back in Pontypandy, Mrs Price and Bella were gossiping outside Mrs Price's store when the kite flew overhead. At that moment, Mrs Price, who missed very little, looked up. "Well I never!" she exclaimed. "Someone's lost their kite."

The kite flew overhead, blown on by the wind, until it became snagged on Mrs Price's television aerial.

"Whatever next?" clucked Mrs Price. "I can't have a kite on my roof ... what will the neighbours say?"

At that moment, Sam and Steele were driving past.

"Sam!" called Mrs Price. "Over here!"

Sam spotted her and pulled Jupiter over. "I wonder what Mrs Price is in such a flap about?" said Sam.

"Perhaps her tongue's on fire from too much gossiping!" chuckled Steele.

Mrs Price explained about the kite, and Steele said, "I'll leave you to deal with it, Sam, while I pop into Bella's for a cuppa."

"Leave this to the fire service, Mrs P," said Sam confidently. "I'll have it down in no time."

Sam put the ladder against the wall and climbed up. "It looks like I'll need to climb on to the roof to reach it," said Sam. But just then, a gust of wind blew the ladder over! "Great fires of London!" cried Sam. "Now what will I do? Oh well, I may as well get the kite while I'm here."

But as he reached out for it, he slipped and fell, just managing to hang on to the aerial.

He was hanging on for dear life when Steele appeared. "Forest fires!" exclaimed Steele in surprise.

Station Officer Steele got the ladder back up, and a relieved Sam climbed down with the kite.

"This looks like James and Sarah's kite," said Sam.

Just at that moment Sarah appeared. "Come quickly, Uncle Sam!" called Sarah. "Mr Evans has hurt his arm!"

Trevor was sitting on the park wall when Sam and Steele arrived with the first aid kit. Steele quickly took command. "Leave this to me," he said confidently. "I'm trained in first aid."

"Yes, but..." said Trevor, as Steele began bandaging.

"No buts," interrupted Steele. "This is a job for experts."

Steele finished bandaging Trevor's arm and patted him on the back. "It's nothing serious," said Steele. "That arm will be fine in no time."

"That arm's fine already," said Trevor indignantly. "It's the other arm that hurts!"

Sam and the children tried not to giggle.

"You can't drive your bus with a sore arm," said Sam.

"No, you can't," said Steele. "I tell you what, I'll drive your bus back to the depot and Sam can give you a lift to the doctor's in Jupiter."

"I'll drop you two children at home, too, if you like," said Sam to Sarah and James.

"But we haven't flown our kite yet," replied Sarah.

"Perhaps I know an easier way of flying it," said Sam.

A curious Sarah and James climbed aboard Jupiter.

Sam drove Jupiter over the hills and valleys of Pontypandy, until a baffled James asked, "Where's the kite, Uncle Sam?"

"Look out of the window," Sam replied.

To their surprise, the children saw their kite tied to the back of Jupiter, flying merrily in the sky!

"I wish I'd thought of that earlier," chuckled Trevor.

They all laughed and laughed.